Taking the Ice

KHALLI'S BIG TEST

Allye M. Ritt

ISBN 978-1-64559-866-4 (Paperback)
ISBN 978-1-64559-867-1 (Digital)

Covenant Books, Inc.
11661 Hwy 707
Murrells Inlet, SC 29576
www.covenantbooks.com

For my skaters…

It is such a privilege to share the skating world with you. Thank you for letting me be a part of your journey!

INTRODUCTION

Ice Rink Life

It's so cold in here! The rink air bites at my face, the only part of me that's exposed. I'm bundled in a fleece jacket, vest, leg warmers, and mittens. As soon as I finish my warm-up, layers will start to come off, and I'll toss my pile of extra clothing on the rink boards, one layer at a time. But not yet!

I push myself across the glass-like ice as I grasp my water bottle tightly through my puffy mittens. Skating takes so much energy, so I've learned to never come to the rink without my water bottle. Today I have a lesson, and I'm pretty sure I could never survive a skating lesson without a full bottle of water. My skating lessons are very intense!

I glance around me as I skate across the ice; some of these skaters are so fast; I really need to make sure I stay out of their way.

There's a girl in the middle spinning faster than my eyes can even move. My eyes feel like they are twitching when I try to follow her spin. One, two, three, four…faster, faster! I can't even count the revolutions anymore because she's spinning so insanely quick!

The boy at the other end of the ice just landed a powerful double jump. His leg is stretched out behind him with a perfectly pointed toe in his shiny black skates. Wow! I can't wait until I can do these things!

Two other skaters are working with their coaches on their technique while another girl is skating to her program music. The stereo volume is nearly maxed out, and the energy of the music makes me want to move with as much strength and emotion as she has. But despite my desire to make up my own movements to her music, I make sure to stay out of her way. Whoever is doing their program has the right of way on the ice.

I take a deep breath as I skate over to the hockey boards where I will set down my water bottle. There's something about the smell of rink air. It's difficult to describe. It kind of smells like a freezer but without the scent of food. It's fresh, crisp, and clean smelling, maybe with a hint of chemical. My dad says he can smell the ice rink in my hair after a day of training. I can't tell if he's right or not; I definitely don't smell the ice rink on me.

At 8:00 a.m., my lesson will begin. This means I only have about ten minutes to warm up beforehand. Once my lesson starts, I need to be ready to push myself; my muscles will do that much better when they are warm. Warm muscles are also more flexible, and flexibility is key in figure skating. Some of the skills I am practicing now require more flexibility than I have ever used before in my life. I feel awkward doing these bendy-type movements, but the other skaters tell me skating will feel more and more natural the longer I do it. I sure hope so!

I set my water bottle on the boards and skate off to get warm. Ten minutes is enough time as long as I use my time wisely. I can't wait for my lesson when I can show my coach how hard I've been practicing!

CHAPTER 1
Practice Makes...Pain

"Keep your knee straight, point your toe, *hold it...hold it...* almost there...okay good. You can put your leg down."

I hate spirals! Coach Marie always makes me stretch my spirals at the rink boards before I can do them on the ice. She says I need to build my strength—spirals are like arabesques in dance; they basically are like doing the splits with one leg standing on the ground while one leg is aiming upwards. Spirals are miserable to learn!

To stretch my spiral position, Coach Marie pushes one of my feet up behind my head while making sure both of my knees are straight. She guides me in adjusting my shoulders, hips, and back, so that everything is in the right place. It's crazy how picky she can get!

"These are looking so much better Khalli!" Coach Marie encourages me. "You're really getting stronger and more flexible. Let's try them moving now."

As I skate across the ice in my spiral position, with one leg stretched up as high as it goes behind me, Coach Marie records me with her iPad.

"Not bad, Khalli! Come take a look."

I skate over to my coach and lean over her iPad. Wow! I really look like an actual figure skater now! My blonde ponytail flows in the wind on the iPad screen making me look fast and powerful. And my spirals are so much better already! I've spent so much time stretching my legs and holding the proper position at home. It's been a lot of work but totally worth it now that my spiral looks so good! If I can get my other skills just as good, I'll be ready for my first test!

Coach Marie has been helping me work towards my very first skating test. My lessons are exhausting, but I'm getting so much better. There are other skaters at my rink who have already passed six or more tests; I want to be as good as they are. Coach Marie says they all started at this same beginning level.

When becoming a good figure skater, you need to take tests to show your progress. The tests are judged by real judges (like the kind you see at the Olympics!), who want to help skaters grow. I'm practicing really hard for my first NOISE Skating Skills test.

NOISE is the National Organization of Ice Skating Education—it's basically like the school principal of figure skating. It makes all of the rules. NOISE also controls competition rules and even decides who is going to get to go to the Olympics. Taking my level one Skating Skills test is the first step in becoming a real figure skater! I want to pass this test so badly. I can't stop thinking about it!

"Show me your entire pattern now."

Coach Marie wants me to skate my spirals one after another, as if one spiral isn't exhausting enough! *Ugh*! I start at the edge of the rink and push really hard so I have enough speed. Up with the leg! I push it as high as it goes and squeeze my knee straight just like Coach Marie told me to.

"Keep your chin up! Pull up to create an arch in your back!" I hear her calling, but that scares me. I feel safer when I see the ice below me. It makes me feel in control when I can see the ice speeding past below me, and I like to watch—*boom*!

Not again! I tripped over my toe pick and crashed super hard onto my knees and stomach. I don't even want to move, it hurts so much! My tummy is aching from the fall, and I can hardly breathe. Spiral falls are the absolute worst!

Coach Marie rushes over to me and crouches down next to me to make sure I'm okay. I insist I am even though it hurts so badly. I wipe the burning tears from my eyes and take my coach's hand. She pulls me up, and we glide slowly over to the bench together. I feel even more pain when I try to sit, bending my knee is apparently a bad idea. After a couple minutes of rubbing my knees, I decide it's time to stop being a baby. The more advanced skaters get up after they fall—so should I!

"Your spirals are getting really strong." Yana smiles as she stops by the boards to get a drink of water. "What's your name?"

I beam back at her. I can't believe she noticed me! Yana is one of the best skaters at the rink; she can do two double jumps already and is working on her third, the double loop. I can't even do a single loop very well yet. In addition to being a beautiful skater, I also think she's one of the prettiest girls at Berger Lake Ice Center. She has gorgeous long wavy black hair with big warm honey-colored eyes. Her skin is dark and smooth, like milk chocolate. Yana also has the biggest smile of anyone I've ever met and as talented, beautiful, and cool as she is, she just noticed me!

"Khalli, my name is Khalli Davies. You're Yana, right?"

"I am. Ka-Lee." She sounds out my name. "That's pretty!"

"Thank you!"

"You're welcome! Hey, about your spirals… Just don't forget to keep your chin up and keep that upward pull all the way through your shoulders and into your back. That will help keep you from falling forward and tripping over your toe picks. But we've all taken a fall like that, falling is all part of the learning process."

I thank Yana for her advice and tell Coach Marie I'm ready to try again. I'm a little nervous as I repeat my spiral pattern, but now that I know what I did wrong, I'm confident I can fix it.

"Way better, Khalli!" my coach cheers. "You kept your chin up and your knees weren't even the slightest bit bent." She reminds me again to point my toe, and we go on to the next pattern for my test.

When my lesson is over, I have another thirty minutes to practice. I spend my time working on everything Coach Marie helped me improve, but I work the hardest on my spirals. They are so close to being good enough to test, and I really want to get to the next level. I can do this!

*****

After my lesson, Mom picks me up.

"Did you see my spirals today?" I ask excitedly.

"Just the last few at the end. Your toe is still flexed and pointed down towards the ice, didn't Marie tell you to fix that?"

Seriously? Why didn't Mom notice that my knee wasn't bent or that my leg was higher? She has no idea how difficult these are; she's never even tried them. And then to do them with skates on! She doesn't understand how hard I'm trying. I start telling her how much better they are, but I'm so frustrated I can hardly get the words out.

Mom's face suddenly softens. "I'm so sorry, honey. I know you're working really hard, and I love your progress. I did see that your leg was higher, and you look much stronger. I was just trying to help. I know how badly you want to take this test and that the spirals are the hardest part for you. You're doing a good job, Khalli. You really are!"

I try to smile. I know I shouldn't be mad at Mom; she was trying to help. But I wanted her to celebrate with me. I guess it's not time to celebrate my spirals yet. If my mom can see my mistakes, then the judges certainly can as well.

I sit quietly the rest of the drive home, thinking about what I need to do to make these spirals perfect. I can fix my toe point, I just need to remember to think about it while I'm thinking about everything else, like my shoulders, my knees, my chin, my core muscles. It really is so much work!

When we get home, I run to my room and practice my spiral position in my mirror. Grandma and Grandpa bought me an extra big mirror for my bedroom, so I can practice my positions and watch myself. I pay extra attention to my toes. I'm going to fix this before my next lesson. I can do this!

CHAPTER 2

Purple Knees

"Khalli, get up! It's already 5:30 a.m., and you have a 6:00 a.m. lesson."

I open my eyes to my mom; she looks as tired as I feel. My whole body aches from yesterday's fall; I'm afraid to move. I start wiggling my toes; they seem okay. Next, I roll my ankles into little circles, also fine. Feeling confident that my body is tough enough, I swing my legs over the side of the bed. And then I feel it! The skin on my knees pulls tightly over my muscles and bones as I bend; it throbs like crazy! Looking down, I glare at where the pain is coming from—my purple knees. Both of them. These are the biggest bruises I've ever had!

Mom sees me looking down and sneaks a peak. I hear her wince, but she quickly tries to cover up her surprise. She fails.

"Khalli, honey. Maybe you should stay home today and let your body rest. I will call Marie and tell her not to expect you for a lesson."

"No. I'm going. I fixed my spiral in my mirror last night, and I want to show Coach Marie. I want to know if I fixed everything correctly, and I'll only know if I have a lesson. And besides, if you cancel last minute, you still have to pay for Coach Marie's time. So please just let me go skating, Mom."

Mom smiles. "You're just like your father, so stubborn. But you are also hard working, I love that about both of you."

I grin back. I'm going to the rink!

Mom helps me get ready. I grab a homemade granola bar and a banana for breakfast to eat in the car on the way.

I put my skates in the trunk along with my school bag because Mom will take me straight to school after practice. It's going to be a long day.

At the rink, I'm really rushed. I only have five minutes to get my skates on if I want to warm up before my lesson. There are four other girls already on the ice. I really should get here earlier if I want to skate as well as them. I tell myself that tomorrow I'll get up earlier, by myself. Mom shouldn't need to wake me; this is my dream.

When I get on the ice, I find myself hesitant. I really don't want to fall again. I do my warm up at a slower speed; I need to watch out for those toe picks! After warming up, I head back to the rink boards to stretch. Yana is stretching right next to me.

"I see you're back for more! How are you feeling after that fall?" she asks me.

I shyly tell her about my purple knees.

"Battle scars," she says boldly. "I have lots of them but every single one of them tells a story. The bruises fade, but some of the cuts will remain. When I look at the scars, they remind me of how hard I've worked, how far I've come, and how I am earning my success."

Yana points to a scar on her elbow. "My axel. Man, I worked hard to land that. I crashed into the ice elbow first for this one." Then she points to her finger. "Biellmann spin. I tried to grab my foot and nicked my finger pretty aggressively with my blade; there was so much blood. But that spin is so gorgeous now, totally worth the effort! You'll get more, and they'll always hurt. Just remember it's part of the process, and it'll be worth it in the end. Every time!"

How cool! I just earned my first battle scar! I'm one of them now, one of the serious figure skaters! I don't really want the pain of earning more. However, if I want to be a good skater like Yana, I know I need to learn to get up after even the toughest falls.

Coach Marie skates over to us. "Nice job yesterday, Yana! I hope to see more double loops from you today!"

"You landed your double loop?!" I ask excitedly.

"Six of them," Yana boasts.

"Six *clean* double loops," Coach Marie adds.

"You should see my purple knees," Yana smiles. Then she winks at me, "Totally worth it."

I look at the clock. It's already 6:00 a.m. I wish I would have woken up a little sooner; I want a few more minutes to try my spirals before I show my coach. I want them to be perfect, but it's too late. It's time for my lesson.

"Let's start with your stroking today. I want to warm you up a little more before we stretch your legs for the spirals."

Coach Marie must have noticed I got here at the last minute. Even though I feel like I failed for not warming up enough on my own, I'm relieved she's starting me with something less aggressive than spirals. Stroking isn't easy, but it's not as difficult as the spirals are for me.

Stroking is just pretty forward skating, but for some reason it doesn't feel nearly as effortless as it looks. Coach Marie has asked me to work on my extension. She wants my free leg lifted higher behind me and my toe pointed. She's really picky about toes. However, her skaters are the prettiest, most graceful skaters at the rink, so that must be why, because she's so picky.

"That extension looks so much better, Khalli! You've really put some effort into it. I love that you aren't pushing off the ice with your toes anymore, and you're getting so much more power!" She makes me repeat the stroking pattern in the other direction. Man, this pattern is mentally exhausting when I think about everything from my toes, to my knee bend, to my extension, my posture, my everything. Sometimes I forget to breathe when I'm so busy thinking, and Coach Marie needs to remind me. It's just overwhelming.

Coach Marie gives me several tips and tells me to work more on my stroking during my own time. How am I getting homework for skating? It's my favorite type of homework, though, and I promise her I'll work on it. I'm so excited to work on my spirals with her. I hope she notices that I fixed them.

"Show me your spiral pattern," she tells me. Wait. What? Don't I have to stretch the spirals on the wall first? When I ask Coach Marie, she tells me the best news yet. "Your flexibility has improved so much, and I already saw you stretching on your own today. I'm confident you might be ready to try this without working through it at the boards first. Let's see!"

I hope I don't disappoint her. I take a deep breath and start my pattern. I feel a little shaky when I push onto my second foot; this is where I fell yesterday. Chin up, chin up, I tell myself over and over. Point the toes. Almost there. Whew! I finished the pattern without falling, and I think I even remembered to do everything my coach told me.

"Nice job, Khalli! That is so much better than yesterday! What did you do to fix it?"

I tell her how I worked in front of the mirror last night, and she gives me the biggest high five. "Your work ethic is going to get you somewhere, Khalli. Keep it up. I have big goals for you."

I beam back at her. I did it!

"I still need you to make one little adjustment." *Ugh.* Really? I thought it was better. "I need you to get your left leg just a little bit higher. Your free leg needs to be at hip level or higher. It's a little too low still."

"How much too low?" I ask. She shows me at the boards. Man! I really thought my leg was higher than that. It feels like it's up in the clouds; I'm working so hard!

Coach Marie makes me stretch my spirals at the boards anyway. I feel her pushing against my leg to make it go higher. I really don't think it'll go up any higher. When I've reached my max, she makes me hold it.

"Ten, nine, eight, *sev-ven, siiix, fiiive…*" She is counting slower and slower. "*Fouuurrr…*" my leg is shaking, I don't know how much longer I can hold it up. "*Threee, twooo,* one!" My leg drops as I gasp for air.

"Were you holding your breath the entire time? You really need to breathe."

"Sorry." I make a mental note to breathe next time.

We do the other leg the same way. This one is much easier for me. After stretching, we repeat the pattern, and I nailed it!

"Best one yet, Khalli!" Coach Marie does a little celebration dance for me. I giggle, but on the inside, I feel so proud of myself.

"Let's go on to freestyle for the rest of your lesson." My favorite words! I love freestyle! The jumps, the spins, all of it! Coach Marie is getting me ready for my first skating program with music. I literally cannot wait!

CHAPTER 3

Spirals Aren't the Only Thing that Requires Balance

"Mom! I had the best lesson ever! I did my spirals the best yet, and we started learning the sit spin!"

"I saw! You did so well this morning," my mom cheers.

"I can't wait for my next lesson," I tell my mom as I take my skates off. "Can I practice tomorrow morning even though I don't have a lesson. Coach Marie gave me homework, and I really want to fix everything before I see her again."

My mom sighs. "Do you really want to get up at 5:30 a.m. when you don't have a lesson?"

"I do, Mom, I really do."

"Tell you what, if you can wake yourself up, I'll take you. Prove to me that you really want this."

"Deal!" I'm going to need to set about six alarms, but it'll be worth it.

*****

When I get to school, I grab my backpack from the trunk and race inside. I skated until the last minute, and now I need to run to class. As I rush through the door to my fifth grade class, Mrs. Hill gives me the look. Shoot. No running in school. At least I'm not late.

I slide into my seat just as the bell rings and prepare myself for a math lesson. I wish math was as fun as skating. At least I can do my homework for math anywhere though, getting to the ice rink to do my skating homework requires a little more organizing. Thankfully, my mom really supports my goals. She said as long as my grades are good, I can keep skating as much as I want. This means I can never slack off in school.

During recess, I ask to stay inside.

"Aren't you coming outside?" Becky and Dacia ask. "We didn't see you outside before school either. We are playing tag by the monkey bars. It's your favorite!"

"I want to finish as much homework as I can. If I don't have to do it at home, I can spend more time working on my skating positions in front of the mirror."

"When did you get so obsessed?" Becky frowns.

"I just want to pass this first skating test, that's all. And then I'll come play."

Becky and Dacia head outside, and Mrs. Hill takes a seat next to me.

"Khalli?"

"Yes, Mrs. Hill?"

"I think it's fantastic that you care so much about getting good grades and about skating. However, it's also important that you make time for your friends and that you find time for fun."

"But skating is fun! It's work, but I really enjoy it. It's what I want to do more than anything else in the world. I'd even rather skate than play tag with Becky and Dacia, and tag used to be my favorite thing in the world!"

Mrs. Hill smiles. "Okay, Khalli. Let's make a deal. I'll let you do homework inside for one recess each day as long as you agree to go outside and play for the other recess. Balance."

"Deal." I really like Mrs. Hill. I don't really know exactly what she means by balance, but it sounds like a good thing to me.

CHAPTER 4

ROTFL

After school, I walk home with Becky. She lives just down the street from me. Dacia takes the bus home, so we usually don't get to see each other after-school. It's nearing the end of our Wisconsin winter, so we are really bundled up: puffer jackets, mittens, hats, boots—the whole nine yards.

"My parents said if I get good grades this quarter, I can get a hamster!" Becky exclaims. "I want a girl hamster. What do you think I should name her?"

"Hmmm…that's an important decision. What about Sasha? Or Alina? Mirai?" I suggest some of my favorite skaters' names to her.

"I was thinking something more fun. Like Sparkles, Hammy Poo, SterSter, or Fluffy Cheeks."

"Those are some of the best Hamster names I've heard! What else were you thinking?"

"That's why I asked you, Khalli, duh!" she giggles.

"What about Green Eggs and HAMster or Scalloped Potatoes and HAMster," I quip.

Becky busts out laughing which makes me lose control. Immediately, we're laughing so hard we have to stop walking in order to hold our stomachs. Becky presses her arms against her forest green puffer jacket, mittens disappearing into the poof of her winter gear. Her green eyes sparkle with tears that suddenly burst over her ginger-colored eyelashes and stream down her freckled face. Of course, this makes me laugh even harder. I snort. Now Becky is laughing out of control to the point where she falls on the ground. An elderly lady across the street stares at us. Once we realize how ridiculous we must look to her, we laugh even harder.

My belly hurts. My eyes are running. Neither of us can hardly catch a breath from our giggle spasm.

Becky makes a serious face and takes the deepest inhale I've ever heard. "Oh, that's cold!" She struggles to catch her breath.

I bust out even harder at her failed attempt to stop laughing. Suddenly, Becky starts crawling on her hands and knees towards her house.

"What are you doing!" I snort.

She tries to hold her laughter down as she whimpers. "Too much laughing," she stammers. "Now I have to pee, really, really badly, but I can't stand up."

I can't even take it anymore. I double over and end up rolling on the ground right next to her. My tummy hurts so badly that I can't stand either, and I'm laughing at how silly we are. I love my best friend!

It seems like forever before we finally collect ourselves enough that we can walk the rest of the way home. When we get to her house, which is just a couple minutes before my house on our walk, Becky turns around and gets a really serious look on her face.

"I miss you, Khalli."

"What do you mean. We're together right now. How can you miss me?"

"We used to spend every spare minute together. I saw you more than I saw my own family. But now you're gone all the time. Most of the time when I come over, you're not home. You're always skating. Sometimes I think you like skating more than you like me."

I swallow hard. "I'm sorry, Becky. You know you're my best friend, and I love being with you. But I also love skating, and it also makes me so happy. I don't want you to stop being my friend, however I don't want to stop skating either."

Becky doesn't seem to know what to say. I feel really bad.

"Hey! Maybe you can come skating with me. Then we can spend time together, and we can skate too! That would make me even happier!"

Becky shakes her head. "I tried ice skating. It was kind of fun, but soccer is my sport."

I smile. "And when it's soccer season, you'll be super busy, just like I am now. And we'll still be best friends because we'll both understand that our friendship is strong enough to survive our busy lives."

"You're right. Although I'm still going to miss you until then."

"But we'll still walk home together every day." I promise.

*****

I finish my reading homework and double check that I've completed all of my other assignments. It's only 5:00

p.m., and I'm done with school for the night. I run upstairs to practice my spirals in front of my mirror. *Ugh!* My knee feels straight but it looks bent in the mirror; I've got to fix this! I turn sideways and do another spiral to get a better view. Yes, it's definitely bent. A couple deep breaths and I try again. I squeeze my leg muscles and feel myself pushing my kneecap further into my knee. There! That's it! Perfectly straight! I can't wait to show Coach Marie!

CHAPTER 5

Lost

Beep-beep-beep-beep-beep.

"Ah, already…?" I grumble as I resist from pulling my pillow over my head. What was I thinking? I'm so tired!

I slowly pull my exhausted body out of bed and turn off my alarm. I've got to prove to Mom that I want this enough to wake up on my own. I tiptoe down the hallway to my parents' room. I don't want to wake Dad, but I need to make sure Mom is up and ready. Mom is still asleep. Should I wake her and risk waking Dad? I decide I should. Just as I place my foot in the room I shriek and jump backwards.

Beep-beep-beep.

Mom shoots out of bed, her blonde hair a total mess, and Dad rips his covers off and stares at me.

"Sorry! I was coming to wake you, Mom. I didn't know that you set an alarm, and it scared me when it went off. I didn't mean to scream." Mom starts laughing at me; Dad is still staring.

"Dad! It's just me who screamed. Everything is okay. I'm sorry. Mom's alarm scared me." Dad looks like he's still trying to process everything that just happened.

"So everything's okay?" He asks bewildered.

"Yes, Dad. You can go back to bed. I'm sorry."

Dad sometimes works really late. He picked up extra hours at work so that Mom could be home more. Without Mom to drive, I couldn't get to the rink. Dad says my dreams are really important to him, and it's worth it to see me so happy. If I weren't already a total Daddy's girl, I would be for sure after that! Dad is pretty much the best!

"I'm proud of you for waking up early to chase your goals, Khalli. I can't wait to see you skate again soon. But you're right, I need to go back to bed." Dad pulls his covers over his head.

I bet he'll be snoring again in two minutes, I think to myself as I skip down the hall to get ready. After that moment of panic, I'm wide awake!

*****

At the rink, I am bundled up. It is so cold today. Two jackets, a vest, legwarmers, super thick mittens, and it's still not enough. I'm shivering as I try to warm up. It seems like forever before I'm warm enough to stretch. Coach Marie skates over to me when I'm stretching.

"I'm so happy to see you here practicing even though we don't have a lesson today! And it makes me happy to see you have enough warm clothing! The manager turned up the blowers last night because the ice was really soft. Soft ice happens if the air is too warm. The blowers make the cold air flow more. The ice is definitely frozen rock hard again this morning." She says through shivering teeth.

Maybe I should have slept in today I think to myself. No no no! I catch myself right away and make myself think positively. If I want to pass this test, I need to practice.

I start with my stroking pattern. It's getting easier and easier. I really hope it looks better. Next, I run through the rest of my patterns for my test, saving my spirals for last.

"Those look even better today! Almost there!" Yana calls as she skates past me.

Almost there? How much better do they need to be, I wonder to myself. They are still really hard, and I question if they'll ever be good enough. After three patterns of spirals, I take a break and move on to my spins. I'm really excited about my new skill—the sit spin. Even though it's really difficult, it's my new favorite thing.

Another skater, Stacy, is also in the middle working on spins. She is such a beautiful skater! I hope I can spin like her someday. I stare in amazement at her speed and control.

"Excuse me!"

Whoa! Oops! I was so busy watching Stacy that I didn't even notice Tamerah flying by. Tamerah is the absolute best skater at Berger Lake Ice Center. She's so fast and powerful; I should have been paying better attention. I skate to the wall embarrassed. Maybe I'm not good enough to be out here yet.

"Don't worry about her," Yana skids up next to me. "She's crabby today because she lost her double axel... again."

"She lost it? Where did it go? I don't get it."

Yana laughs at me. "It's just a saying in skating. When you can do something and then suddenly you can't, we say we lost it. It just means you're in a slump. It's not gone forever; skills come back. But as of this week, Tamerah can't do her double axel anymore."

"Oh." I feel bad for Tamerah. I hope I never lose my spiral!

*****

After the session ends, I take my skates off next to Stacy. Stacy is tiny and therefore looks much younger than she is. I think she's actually about fifteen, but I'm not positive. She has pale skin and bright blue eye. Her long blonde hair is usually in pigtail French braids which flair out when she spins. It's really cool to watch!

"I've seen you here a lot lately, Khalli! Coach Marie says you're a hard worker and that you'll go far. It's good that you're working with her, she's a great coach!"

"Thank you! I love your spins!" I shyly reply.

Stacy beams. "Spinning is my favorite part of skating. Some skaters like jumping, some like dance and footwork, me, I love to spin!"

I wonder what I'll be best at. I start thinking about all of the skills and imagining myself doing them.

"Are you going to do the ice show this year?" Stacy interrupts my thoughts.

"Ice show?"

"Yeah, every season we hold a big ice show. Skaters perform solos, duets, big group numbers, and more. It's our chance to show what we've learned to our families and friends, and it's so much fun! You should think about it. It's not for a couple months, but you should probably talk to Coach Marie about it soon if you're interested."

"Thanks! I will!" I can't wait to tell my mom about this! I can be in an ice show!

CHAPTER 6

Learning Focus

On the way to school, I excitedly tell Mom about the ice show. She has a million questions for me, and I really don't have any answers.

"I just know I really want to do it! I want to show everyone what I've been working on and why I've been at the rink so much."

Mom agrees to message Coach Marie and find out some more details. My biggest concern: "Ask her if I get to wear a skating dress! I really want one!"

Mom smiles knowingly as she drops me off in front of school. I grab my bag from the trunk and skip inside. I might get to be in an ice show!!

My first school lesson today is social studies. We are talking about early American explorers like Sacagawea, Lewis, and Clark. I love history! It reminds me that an ordinary person can make a difference and change the world. How cool that a teenage girl guided grown men through the Rocky Mountains with her husband and baby! How strong and intelligent she must have been!

Maybe I can portray her in the ice show! I could wear a Native American style dress, maybe put my hair in braids. Ooh, and I'll want a feather! What kind of music would I skate to? Could I make my skates look like moccasins? Could I possibly design my entire costume myself? Maybe I should—

"And what is the reason for the Lewis and Clark Expedition, Khalli?"

"What? Ummm, I'm sorry, Mrs. Hill. Can you repeat that?"

"I will. And you will also stay after class. It's important that you pay attention during history."

"I know, I'm sorry."

Mrs. Hill repeats her question and calls on Dacia this time.

"It was to explore the new land in the west and to find a route to the ocean."

"Exactly, Dacia! Who can tell me which ocean?"

I shoot my hand up as fast as I can. Maybe if I answer this I won't get in trouble for daydreaming. Mrs. Hill gives me a chance.

"The Pacific!"

"You're correct, Khalli. However, we are still going to talk after class."

I hang my head. I should have been paying attention. But how did she know I wasn't? Is it that obvious?

*****

When my friends go out to recess, I wait for Mrs. Hill to tell me my punishment. My mom is going to be so mad. She finishes something at her desk, takes her reading glasses off and untucks her straight black hair from ear, and then slowly approaches me.

"Khalli? Were you thinking about skating instead of paying attention?"

I can't lie. She's completely right.

"I was. I'm sorry. I started thinking I could be Sacagawea in the ice show and started daydreaming about my costume. I'm really sorry. I'll do better next time."

"I know you will. I know you care about your grades. But, when you're at the rink do you think about school?"

"No. I think about skating."

"Good. Then I ask that when you are at school you think about school and when you are at the rink you think about skating. That way you'll be good at both school and skating. Distraction will hold you back. If you practice focusing at school, it will also make you better at focusing at the rink. It's an all-around win."

That makes a lot of sense. I smile and thank Mrs. Hill for her advice and for caring.

"Can I still stay in the rest of recess and finish my homework?"

"As long as you are thinking about school when you are doing your work," she says with a wink.

CHAPTER 7
An Ice Cream Toast

My mom surprises me and picks both Becky and me up after-school.

"Becky, I already talked with your mom, and she said you can join us. We're going to go get ice cream. Would you like to come?"

Mom and Becky's mom are really good friends. They were even friends before Becky and I were born and because of that we get to hang out together a lot.

"Absolutely! My favorite is cookie dough ice cream. Can I get that?" Becky squeals.

"Of course! Throw your bags in the trunk. Let's go celebrate!"

"Celebrate? Why?" I ask.

"Oh, I don't know." Mom says with a teasing smile.

"Well, whatever the reason, I'm in!" Becky cheers.

*****

At Snowtop Cream Shop, we pick up our orders and take them to a corner booth. This is my favorite ice cream place. Mom and Dad usually take me here as a reward for good grades when I get my report card.

"Did my report card come already?" I ask.

"Nope. You haven't been graded for why I'm surprising you. Well, at least not yet." Mom hints.

"What?" Becky and I look at each other confused. She tilts her head so her red curly hair falls over half her face, pulls her eyebrow up, and sticks her tongue out to the side trying to look bepuzzled. I laugh so hard I think that my ice cream might come out of my nose.

"Ohhh! That's so cold!" I exclaim as I whip my hands to my face.

Once again, Becky and I lose control and have another one of our special laughing attacks.

Mom smiles knowingly, her skin creasing joyfully around her brown eyes. She never minds these moments of zero control. Becky and I sometimes imagine our moms together falling apart in laughter just like we do. It's got to be genetic, right?

Once we calm down and go back to enjoying our ice cream, I suddenly remember I still don't know why Mom took us to get ice cream.

Mom seems to have been waiting for this very question when I finally compose myself enough to ask it.

"Are you sure you want to know right now?" Mom teases.

"Yes! Pleaaase!" I nearly beg.

"So I talked to Marie today," Mom begins, drawing out every word. I think she enjoys making me anxious.

"And? Tell me! Why are we celebrating?!" I'm so excited; whatever it is, it has to be good news.

Mom pauses, solely to watch me stress, I believe. "Marie said there's a test session next month."

I hold my breath, please say I'm ready, please say I'm ready, I repeat in my head over and over. It's been three months of hard work; I want to be ready so badly!

"Marie said you can take your level one test at the Carnival Ice Center test session!"

"Yeeesss!" comes blaring out of my mouth, completely unintentionally.

"And..." Mom continues into a pause, combing her blonde hair back with her fingers in a relaxed fashion.

There's more? How does Mom look so calm when this is so important! I can't hardly wait to hear the rest so I don't say a word. I don't want to interrupt Mom—I want to know now!

"The ice show is a few weeks after the test session. Marie said you don't have enough lesson time to prepare successfully for both."

Bummer. Although if I can test, not being able to do the ice show won't be the end of the world, I guess. You can't have it all.

"But," Mom begins again with a smile and pauses just like before.

But what? Okay seriously, it's like Mom planned out this entire conversation to play with my emotions.

"Hurry! Tell me!" I beg.

"But Marie said if you would be willing to do an extra lesson each week, you could be ready for both!"

"*EEEEEE*!" I shriek so loudly that the people ordering at the counter all the way on the other side of Snowtop Cream

Shop turn around and stare. "Sorry," I whisper when I see Mom and Becky staring at me.

"So…can I do the extra lessons Mom? Please!"

"Your dad and I already talked about it. We will find a way to make it work. We are both so very proud of you!"

"That's fantastic! I'm so happy for you! I'm totally bringing Dacia and maybe some other friends to the ice show to see you!" Becky cheers.

Mom watches calmly as I freak out with joy and then Becky hugs me so tightly and we rock back and forth. I love these people!

Once we relax again Mom gets the biggest smile on her face; she's almost bursting at the seams. What is she not telling us?

"Mom! What is it? Tell me! Please!" I beg.

Mom gives me the biggest hug, "I'm so proud of you honey for all of this, however, I still have one more thing that you are going to love, maybe even more!"

"Did you get me a dress?" I ask excitedly.

Mom shakes her head. "I thought we'd pick that out together because you will definitely need a nice dress now. And now the other news… Marie said, if you're interested, there is also a competition the week after our ice show at Carnival Ice Center. She said she can choreograph your ice show program in a way that you can use the same program in the competition the following week."

I'm freaking out. Seriously! I don't even know what to say.

"A speechless Khalli. That's something I've never seen before!" Becky jokes. "I think that means yes."

"I'm not so sure," Mom fakes a concerned face. "I don't think Khalli really likes skating."

I'm struggling to get my words out I'm so excited. "Uwa…I…muu," come out of my mouth. Mom and Becky crack up in laughter at the sounds of my struggle.

More excited, struggle sounds. More laughter from Mom and Becky.

And then finally, "I want to do it! I'm in! I'm so in! I've never been so sure about anything! Oh my God this is the best day of my life!" I manage to say as I gasp for air.

Becky takes a spoonful of her cookie dough ice cream and raises it to her month. "An ice cream toast then! To my best friend who is achieving her dreams!"

"An ice cream toast!" Mom and I cheer.

CHAPTER 8

Dedication

"Khalli! Wake up! You have a lot of work to do today!" Mom shakes me.

"What time is it?" I grumble.

"It's 4:45 a.m. Marie could only get you in for extra ice time if she started earlier in the morning; her schedule was booked."

That's right! Skating! Testing, ice show, competition, everything I've ever wanted! I jump out of bed ready to go.

"Wow! If you only woke up that excited about school!" Mom jokes.

*****

I get to the rink early enough to fully warm up and stretch before my lesson. Yana is the only other person on the ice.

"I didn't expect anyone else to be here yet. It's usually empty at this time." She tells me as I stretch on the boards. "Coach Marie wasn't kidding when she said you had big goals!"

"Next month, I'm taking my level one test!" I boast.

"Already? Wow! Get it Khalli! Most skaters spend twice as long preparing for their first test. Then again, you're here just as much as the upper level skaters lately. More practice, more progress! Just like Coach Marie always says."

"She must be right! I didn't expect to be testing so soon!" I say with glee.

"Chitchatting won't make you into stronger skaters." Coach Marie cuts into our conversation. "If you're not stretching or getting a drink, you shouldn't be at the boards."

"I know. And you're absolutely right. I have double flips to be working on."

Yana skates over to one of the hockey lines she has been using to set up her jump.

"And that's how you improve." Coach Marie acknowledges Yana's dedication with a grin. "Let's get to work on your test, and then I have some music selections for you to listen to."

"I'm going to get music already?" I wasn't expecting this to move so quickly. I can't wait to hear what my coach has picked out for me!

"I want to get started right away because we are going to need a lot of time to do this right. Performing isn't just about learning a routine; it's about perfecting it. You'll need to build your strength and endurance so that you can push through one minute and thirty seconds of music. As you improve, your program will get longer. By the senior level, you'll have a four-minute program packed with double and triple jumps, as well as combination spins and footwork; but for now, a minute and a half will do. The more you practice your program, the more it will flow. Our goal is to make all of your jumps, spins, and skills connect together so that your skating program is one fluid work of art. Regular practice is the only way you'll make that happen."

"How long will it take me to learn my program?"

"I can't say for sure. This is different for every skater. It will depend greatly on how easy you find the connections and skills; however, it will also depend on how you learn. Some skaters need a lot of repetition, other skaters are very visual while others learn best by drawing their program or by writing out the order. Through this process, we'll likely figure out how you learn best and then your next program will be easier to learn because we'll know what works best for you going into it."

I hope I'm a quick learner. I'm worried Coach Marie might get frustrated with me. I've never learned this much body movement all at once before. I hope she's as patient as she is when she teaches me other things!

"Will we start learning today already?" I question.

"Not yet. We'll just listen to some music at the end of your lesson. If you like any of the songs, I will cut the music to the correct length and then we'll probably begin next week already. If you don't like any of the choices I have today, don't worry, we can look into more options. We want to pick music that will fit your skating style, but also something that you like. It's also really important that you enjoy the music that you're skating to because you are going to hear it hundreds of times over the next year."

It makes me happy that Coach Marie cares that I will like my music. I like the idea of having input!

"Let's worry about the music later. Right now, I want to work on your skills for the test as well as your loop-loop combination and flip jump. We have a lot of work to do in the next couple months. Let's start with your stroking pattern. Make sure you are thinking about your extension and toe point. Go show me your pattern."

"Okay." I say over my shoulder as I skate to my starting position. I can't believe I'm going to be testing this in a month already!

I do my pattern as best as I can and skate back to Coach Marie. On the way, I try to read her face. Did she like what I showed her?

"Not bad, Khalli. You've definitely been working on the extension and the toe point, but what did I tell you about toe pushes?"

I knew I was forgetting something!

"I'm not supposed to dig my toe pick into the ice when I push. I should turn my foot sideways more, then I can push off more of my full blade, not just my toe."

"Exactly. Toe pushes are a cause to not pass this test. It's very important that you fix this. I know you can. You had really nice pushes in our last lesson. I want you to do it again; this time fix your pushes."

I skate back to my starting position to repeat the entire pattern. On my way, I glance at the clock: 5:37a.m. I could tell Coach Marie that I messed up because I'm so tired, and I'm still not used to getting up this early, but I don't think it will matter. She doesn't like excuses, and I don't think she will be impressed at all. But I do know what will impress her, fixing my toe pushes. And that's exactly what I intend to do.

CHAPTER 9

The Sleepover

After school Becky and Dacia surprise me. How did they keep this a secret all day at school!

"I'm walking home with you," Dacia excitedly announces carrying an extra bag and her pillow. And then we are having a Friday night slumber party at Becky's! Becky's mom already checked with your mom. She said you don't skate until 10:00 a.m. tomorrow. So do you want to join us?"

"Yes!" I practically scream.

"Really? I thought you'd rather practice your skating stuff at home instead," Dacia jeers.

"Wait. Are you mad at me? I thought you just invited me?"

Becky shoots Dacia a mean look.

"What now? You're going to take her side?"

"I am." Becky stands up for me. "I set this up so we could all hang out together. I miss seeing you both. If you're going to be a bully, then you can go home, Dacia. This is supposed to be fun. I will not fight tonight."

Wow! When did Becky get so mature? I have a fantastic best friend!

Dacia looks both mad and embarrassed. She says nothing as we continue our walk home.

"When we get home, I'll run and double check with my mom that it's okay if I sleep over, as long as you want me there." I shoot Dacia a questioning look.

Dacia still says nothing and just continues walking with us. Her dark brown hair folds slightly over her porcelain face as she hangs her head in embarrassment. Dacia is really pretty, even when she's mad. Her perfectly straight dark hair sparkles in the sun making her look like she's radiating happiness, which seems weird to me right now as she's pouting.

Becky and I begin talking about what movies we are going to watch and what we want on our pizza. Dacia always reacts this way when she feels bad. We've learned to give her space and let her join us again when she feels ready.

*****

Once we reach my driveway, I bolt into the house to check with Mom. She agrees, of course, but jokes that it's only okay if she can have a sleepover with Becky's mom next week.

I grab my clothes and pillow and run back to Becky's house. Mom is going to pick me up at 9:00 a.m. with my skates and everything I'll need for the rink.

I run up Becky's steps and straight through the door. We never knock at each other's houses. Our moms say we are family and that means we are welcome anytime. Becky and I of course think this is fantastic.

"Hi, Auntie Liz!" I announce as I run through the kitchen and up the steps. Auntie Liz isn't of course my real aunt, but I've called her Auntie since I was able to talk. My mom doesn't have any sisters and says that Auntie Liz is just like a sister to her. Works for me!

"I'm here!" I announce as I slide into a spot on the floor next to Becky and Dacia.

"Whoa! Watch out!" Becky screams as she pulls her feet off the floor two inches from where I slide. "My toe nail polish is perfect; and if you wreck it, my pedicurist is going to get crabby." She winks at Dacia who is still holding the nail polish brush in her fingers.

"Take your shoes off and pick your color! I hereby cordially apologize for being mean and am performing pedicures in an act of love," Dacia professionally announces.

I have the weirdest friends! But, man, they are fantastic!

"And you are obviously forgiven!" I joyfully announce with an attempt to be as professional sounding as Dacia.

"Cha Cha Fuschia, Pink Tutu, or Matcha Latte?" I ask reading the bottoms of the Becky's nail polish.

"All of them!" Becky squeals.

"You are creating a difficult customer." Dacia keeps her serious, professional voice on. "A single color would accent your…your…ummm…your skin tone better."

Becky and I burst out in laughter at Dacia trying to be so official.

"Stop!" Dacia fires a look at Becky. "You will bump your toes if you keep rolling on the ground in a giggle fit and will ruin my masterpiece." She maintains perfect professionalism through her entire sentence.

It's over for me now. "*HURRNNNNNCKK*," I snort. Followed by "*HURNCHHHHH, HUUURNK.*"

Dacia and Becky squeal as soon as the snorts come out. Tears come running down my face from laughing so hard and Dacia doubles over onto the bed holding her stomach. I have the greatest friends ever!

*****

"A Disney movie or a scary movie?" Becky asks as we are cleaning up our pizza mess.

"Scary!" Dacia and I both shout at the same time.

"That's what I was hoping for!"

We search Netflix for the perfect choice and finally settle on *The Ring*. Auntie Liz says we aren't allowed to watch anything above PG-13, but thankfully there are still a lot of choices. I hope this one is scary enough to keep me awake; my eyes are already feeling heavy.

We made a blanket fort on Becky's bedroom floor, and Auntie Liz gave us her big-screen laptop to set up inside as our television. As we are skipping through the previews, the smell of warm buttered popcorn fills the air.

"Is it safe to come in?" Becky's older brother Rudy asks.

Rudy is home for the weekend from college and is really the coolest boy I've ever met. Most big brothers act like they hate their little sisters, but Rudy is the absolute opposite. Maybe it's because he's so much older than Becky, but he genuinely loves making Becky happy and helps her with anything he can.

"Absolutely!" We chant together.

"I can't stay. Like Mom said, I have a paper to write this weekend, but I thought I'd bring you some freshly made, gourmet popcorn with extra butter. Scary movies are always better when you have something to eat during the horror scenes."

"Thank you!" We all sing together as Rudy drops off the popcorn.

"Auntie Liz planned this sleepover so you wouldn't bother Rudy while he works, didn't she?" I ask.

"I hadn't thought about it, but you're probably right. I hope Rudy gets more homework next time he's home!" Becky jokes.

CHAPTER 10

The Perfect Pose

"Wake up, Khalli!" Becky is shaking me. Your mom will be here soon, and breakfast is ready downstairs.

"Is it morning already?" I ask groggily. "What time did we go to bed?"

"We went to bed around 1:00 a.m. You passed out ten minutes into the movie and snored through the entire thing."

"*Ugh*! I'm so sorry!"

"It's fine. Dacia and I had fun painting your face after you passed out."

"What!" I jump out of bed and run to the bathroom to check the mirror. I hope I can get it off before Mom takes me to the rink.

When I see my reflection, I have to blink a couple times. I stare into my dark brown eyes. I don't see anything but myself.

Becky and Dacia are giggling in the hallway.

"Kidding! But now we are even for you falling asleep so early!"

"Oh, we're not even! I am so getting you back!" I joke as I race to get ready.

*****

At the rink, I have an hour lesson with Coach Marie. We spend thirty minutes working on my test and then she surprises me.

"I cut the music you picked out already and am prepared to start your program. Would you like to start today?"

"Yes!" I start jumping up and down but quickly realize this level of excitement feels very different with skate blades on my feet.

Coach Marie giggles, her hazel eyes sparkling, as I catch my balance with a shocked look on my face.

"It's the song from *Moana*, right?" I confirm.

"No…I thought you picked the music from *Avengers*. Shoot, did I cut and choreograph the wrong song?"

My heart sinks, I don't want Coach Marie to have to do extra work, but I also really wanted to skate to *Moana*.

"I'm just kidding! Of course, it's the song from *Moana*!"

Coach Marie has the ability to pretend she's serious when she's joking. She fools her skaters every time.

"*Ugh!* Really! Not funny, but I'm really glad it is the right song!" I try to frown in frustration but fail because I'm smiling so much about starting my program today.

"We are going to start with your beginning pose. You'll begin at a hockey dot."

Coach Marie skates over to one of the big red dots in the ice.

"This will make it easy for you to start your program at any rink where you are competing. Almost all rinks have these dots in the ice because they need them for hockey games."

My coach shows me my entry position. She stretches her right leg behind her and points her toe into the ice. Her left arm makes a gentle circle in front of her while her right arm stretches out to the side. Both of her hands are soft and delicate while her head tilts gently to the side, her auburn hair falling over her right shoulder. She instantly looks like a ballerina, like she belongs in a snow globe! I can't wait to try this position. I try to mirror her.

She laughs.

"What?"

"The focused look on your face is hilarious! Don't worry, though. I'll help you make this position possible. The more you do it, the easier it will get, and then you won't need to focus so hard."

Thank goodness. This better be the hardest part! I wonder what is coming next.

"I want you to point your toe and let it rest in the ice behind you. Hold on to me for balance, I'm going to adjust your foot placement a little."

"Whoa!" I collapse against Coach Marie as I lose my balance. How am I supposed to stand like this? My coach takes my left hip and softly pushes it towards my right side a little.

"You want to make sure you don't drop your left hip. Even if you do find a way to balance that way, it will ruin your lines."

"My lines?"

"Think of your body as a silhouette. You want the outer lines of your silhouette to be gentle curves; we don't want bumps all over your silhouette. Everything should be smooth."

"That makes sense." I say as I adjust my lower body.

"Much better! Now for the arms...pretend your left arm is hugging a big beach ball in front of your body. You don't want too much bend in the elbow."

Okay. Beach ball. I can do this.

"Nice, Khalli!" Coach Marie cheers. "If you can relax your hand and fingers, this arm will be good."

"Let's work on your right arm now." She gently takes my right hand and stretches it out past my right side. "I want the softest bend in your elbow. Barely bent, but also not straight. Just like this."

She adjusts my arm as she's talking. I feel a little bit like a doll being positioned during play. But I also feel really pretty and delicate. I wonder if I look as graceful as Coach Marie did doing this position.

"Now the head." Marie softly adjusts my head position so I'm looking upward, just over my left shoulder. I can't believe how hard it was to get in this position!

"Perfect! Stay right there!"

Coach Marie pulls out her iPad and snaps a picture. I feel like I am going to fall over.

"Hurry!" I beg as I feel my body wiggling. I feel like the leaning tower of Pisa, ready to topple any minute!

"You can relax now. I'll send this picture to your Mom after our lesson so that you can practice holding this position in front of your mirror at home. With as hard as you work, I bet it'll be better already by our next lesson." She smiles at me.

"Let's start the next part of your program now!"

Coach Marie and I work on my program through the rest of my lesson. We have about thirty seconds finished, and I already have two jumps and a spiral in my program. I'm so glad I've been working so hard on these spirals!

CHAPTER 11

The Best Surprise

Three weeks later

The day after tomorrow is testing day! I'm so incredibly nervous. Coach Marie said I should test in a dress, and Yana has loaned me one of hers to wear. It's a basic, but incredibly pretty, black velvet dress with some crystals on the skirt and around the waist. Coach Marie has had me practice in it twice now, just so I can get use to the way it feels. I find my legs feel quite different in tights as compared to pants; it's much colder and it feels very breezy!

In my lesson today, Coach Marie said I was completely ready. She has made me do several test runs in the last couple weeks to make sure I'm comfortable with the way the test will work.

I've practiced the test in my mind so many times. I will warm up and then get off the ice and wait my turn to test. When it's time to test, I skate over to the judges and introduce myself. I will have only one judge judging me, the other judges will be judging other skaters at the same time. Next, I skate to the edge of the rink and wait until my judge is looking at me. Once he or she is, I begin. My first pattern is stroking. After my stroking pattern, I stop completely and wait for the judges to write their notes. Then I begin my second pattern. I work through all four patterns this way and then I skate back to my coach and wait for my judge. The entire test should take about ten minutes.

It all seems too nerve-racking!

"Khalli, we're here!" Mom says excitedly.

"Where?" I haven't even been paying attention. Since we got in the car after my lesson I've been in a daydream thinking about my test.

Mom smiles with anticipation as I look at the sign on the building in front of us.

Cutting Edge Skating Supplies and Designs by Amy.

"A skate shop? But I don't need new skates—"

"I know, but there might be something else you need or want here."

"Like laces? I do have a small tear in one of them and it's starting to fray… How did you know?" I'm so confused.

"We can pick up a new pair of laces…but I was thinking something more along the lines of a new dress!"

"I get my own dress?" I shriek. "Are you serious! Wow! This is too good to be true!" I jump out of the car and start running to the door.

"Khalli! Wait for me!" Mom laughs.

At the door, I turn around and jump up and down excitedly as my mom catches up.

"Yana's mom said this place has the best skating dresses! You can try them on and if you like one, we can buy it for your test. Then you can also use it for your competition program."

"You are the best mom ever!" I insist.

"Maybe," smiles Mom. "But the dress was actually your dad's idea. We are both so impressed with how hard you are working and want you to feel confident and beautiful during your test. Whatever happens with your test, whether you pass or have a rough day and need to take it again, you've earned your first dress. We are both so proud of you!"

"Thank you, Mom! And thank you for letting me pick out a dress!" I give my mom the biggest hug. "Can we go inside?" I ask as soon as she lets go of me.

"Absolutely!"

Once inside, I can't believe my eyes. There are so many dresses, and the store is so colorful and sparkly. I'm in heaven!

Pinks and blues and greens and yellows and…that one! That one right there! I head straight to a beautiful purple and blue dress with blends of pinks and greens mixed into the colors. Wow!

"This one looks like water on a tropical island!" I swoon. "Just like the water on Moana's island!"

"That's funny you say that. I asked Marie what she would recommend, and she suggested we aim for blue to give the illusion of water. She also said however, as long as you avoid neon colors, it'll probably match your music just fine."

"Can I try it on? Please!" They only have two dresses in that style, and one is exactly my size.

"Of course you can, but why don't you pick out a couple others to take with you in the fitting room?"

There are so many pretty dresses, picking out more shouldn't be a problem. I find a stunning grey and black dress. The top is black, and it fades into a grey skirt with tons of crystals. I also pick out an elaborately designed green and blue dress with a few delicate flowers going across the shoulder and chest. They are all so pretty! How will I choose?

I take all three dresses to the fitting room. Mom takes a picture on her phone of me in each dress so that I can compare the way I look in all three dresses without having to put them all on again.

I save the blue and purple one for last. After I put it on, I turn and face the mirror. I gasp at my reflection. This is it!

"Mom! This is the one I want! Look!"

I twirl my way out of the fitting room with the biggest smile on face.

"Khalli! You look like a princess! Wow! I have such a stunning daughter!" Mom boasts.

I stare at my reflection in the mirror. The top of the dress is a nude-color mesh. The mesh runs across my shoulders and meets the purple velvet which runs across my chest and under my arms. It looks like a strapless dress, except with the mesh top, the dress will be held into place through all of my movement. The deep purple has thin wisps of magenta dyed vertically into the fabric and is heavily decorated with crystals and beading. The purple melts into a bold blue as it reaches my lower ribs. More crystals! The blue continues to fade as it runs down my stomach. At the skirt, it fades into a slightly lighter blue and wisps of green are swirled into the skirt along with light green and blue crystals. The perfect coloring along with the glistening coming off of the crystals give it the appearance of water on a sunny day. Wow!

Mom wipes a tear from her eye.

"Why are you crying, Mom? This is so perfect!"

"That's exactly why I'm crying, Khalli, because this is so perfect!"

Mom doesn't even look at the price tag as she takes it to the register. She sends me over to look at tights and laces while she buys the dress. I see her swallow hard when she's talking to the salesman; but she pulls out her credit card anyway.

"How much was it?" I ask.

"A lot, but it doesn't matter. Dad and I have been saving up for your dress and can afford it. Tamerah's mom warned me about the high prices, so we were prepared. But don't worry about the cost, we both believe you have more than earned your own dress and we want you to have it and we want you to love it. Just…maybe don't grow too much anytime soon." Mom says with a wink.

CHAPTER 12

Necessary Distraction

Tomorrow is testing day! I don't have a lesson, but Mom takes me to the rink anyway after-school. I want to practice one last time and want to run my entire test wearing my new dress, just in case it feels different.

"Khalli! You look beautiful!" Yana skates over to me.

"Thank you! And thank you so much for letting me borrow your dress, but I think it's time for me to give it back. My mom surprised me with my own dress yesterday!"

"I would definitely choose your new dress over mine for the test. It's gorgeous! You can just put my dress by my skate bag if you brought it along today. Do you know which bag is mine?"

"The purple and black one?" I confirm.

Yana nods as she skates off to practice her test. She is taking her level six test tomorrow and has been at the rink daily preparing.

The rink is packed with skaters today, and Coach Marie is wrapped in extra clothing. She often coaches in a jacket, but today she is maxed out in a hat, leg warmers, and a thick scarf. She's wrapped up so much that you can hardly see her auburn hair as it pokes through between her hat and scarf.

Stacy sees me staring at Coach Marie when she comes to the boards to get a drink of water.

"I thought the same thing as you are probably thinking when I came earlier for my lesson. Why is she wearing so many clothes today?"

"I've never seen her so bundled," I reply.

"Coach Marie told me she's been here all day. She has twelve hours of lessons today because of everyone wanting to get one last lesson to calm their nerves before tomorrow's test session. She said she put on more clothing so she could avoid freezing to death," Stacy explains.

"Makes sense. Are you testing?" I ask her.

"I am. I'm really nervous though because I don't feel ready. Coach Marie said my test is very borderline, but she gave me permission to give it a try. I kind of wish I would have chosen to wait." She sighs.

"I'm sure you'll do great!" I encourage her.

"I hope so," she says with a nervous smile and skates away, braids bobbing behind her head.

"Khalli! I love seeing you here! But I noticed you're doing a lot of talking. Make sure if you're here, you're here to skate!" Coach Marie reprimands me.

"I'm sorry. I just bought a forty-five-minute ice session today to try out my dress, and you're right, I should use it."

"That's the Khalli I know!" my coach grins. "Now get to work! And I love your dress!" She says with a wink.

I run through my entire test three times and then practice my spins. Mom asked me not to do anything that might make me fall; she didn't want me to get holes in my new tights or to wreck my dress. I promised to stick to my strengths for today only.

*****

When we get home from the rink, Dad has already made dinner. Chicken stir fry—my favorite! The delicious smell is filling our entire house, and I cannot wait to eat!

"I thought you might need some extra energy for your test tomorrow, and I know you'll eat a double helping of this!"

"Thanks, Dad! I'm so nervous already!"

"I figured you would be, but don't worry, I have the solution for that."

"You do?" I really hope he does!

"When I get nervous for important presentations for work, I do two things. First, I prepare myself to the maximum. You've been skating four times a week for the last several months; you've already done this. Second, I distract myself from thinking about it nonstop. This part I'm going to do for you."

"How?" I question.

"After your gourmet dinner from Chef Dad, I have planned a family game night followed by a movie for you. This is just the cure for your nerves."

I give him a doubting look but agree to give it a try.

"What game?" I ask.

"Guess."

"Monopoly?"

"No."

"Skip Bo?"

"Nope."

"Uno?"

"Also, no."

"Clue?"

"Wrong again."

"Really, Dad! This is so frustrating!" I exclaim.

"But, have you thought about your test in the last twenty seconds?"

"No."

"See! I'm great at distracting you! I bet you even forgot to be nervous!" Dad beams with pride.

"You are so very weird!"

"Thank you! Normal is boring! Now sit down and let's pray together. It's time for your favorite dinner!"

*****

Dad was right! I had so much fun during our family night that I forgot I was nervous about my test until now.

As soon as I turned out my lights and crawled into bed, the busyness of the night had ended. Everything is still and calm, except for my mind.

"What if I fall? What if I fail? What if I forget not to push with my toe? I haven't pushed with my toe in weeks, why would I do it tomorrow? But what if I do? What if my spiral leg isn't high enough? What if I forget my patterns?"

Suddenly I hear Coach Marie's words from my last lesson running through my head. *Khalli, you are totally ready. I have over prepared you. Your skills are above and beyond what is required so even if you make a little mistake, you will still be in a good position to pass. There are no guarantees, but I don't want you to worry. I feel confident you will have a good test, and I need you to also feel confident. You can do this.*

Coach Marie is one of the best coaches in the area. If she thinks I can do this, then I need to believe that I can do this.

I close my eyes and fall asleep to dreams of beautiful spirals in my absolutely stunning dress.

CHAPTER 13

Testing Day

We get to the rink an hour before my test, just like Coach Marie asked. We did my hair at home in a perfect skater-style sock bun. Mom even let me put some light makeup on. Blush, lipstick, and mascara. I think I look very mature!

There are skaters everywhere, many of whom I've never met before. I wonder if most of these skaters are from Carnival Ice Center, or if they are coming from somewhere else, like I am.

Tension fills the air. Most skaters are in colorful dresses and are wearing black warm-up jackets over the top. Some skaters are warming up, others are reading sheets of paper with their coaches; some skaters are celebrating while others are crying. As I scan the crowd, I recognize Yana, Tamerah, and Stacy, as well as several others from Berger Lake Ice Center.

Tamerah is in tears. Her mom and Coach Marie are trying to console her, but it seems useless. Her makeup has run down her normally porcelain-like doll face. Her perfectly positioned braid down the side of her head wraps into a bun with the rest of her dark brown hair; its beauty looks completely out of place next to her face which now looks like it was finger-painted by a small child. She's not wearing her skates but still is in her tights and light pink skating dress. Her long legs look like they go on for days because of the dress' short skirt. I want to tell her how pretty her dress is to make her feel better, but I don't think it will matter. She's holding a crumpled piece of paper in her hands and pushing it back and forth from one hand to the other like she's kneading bread dough.

Yana comes over full of smiles.

"Hey, Khalli! Welcome to your first test session! Coach Marie asked me to help show you around while she talks with Tamerah."

"What happened to Tamerah?" I ask full of concern.

"Tamerah took her gold medal test today. That's the eighth and final level. She didn't pass."

"She didn't pass? But she's the best skater at our rink."

"I thought she looked great out there; and when she got off the ice, she assumed she had passed. She wasn't expecting this at all and is really torn up because it's the first time she's ever failed a skating test."

"But she can take it again, right?"

"She can, and I'm sure she will. But she's been preparing six months for this test and felt really confident. She didn't even mess up, the judges just said it wasn't good enough yet."

"Wow! Poor Tamerah." My nerves just kicked into overdrive. If she didn't pass and she did her best, how can I ever pass?

"She can retest again already in a month if she wants. However, the judges gave her a big list of things she needs to improve, so she might want more time than that. Then again, she might also get different judges next time. Coach Marie said this is a tough group of judges."

"Tough judges?" I ask full of worry.

"I don't think you need to worry, Khalli. Your test looks solid. Now, Coach Marie asked me to help you get ready, so now it's time to focus. She'll be over here in a little."

"Okay." I give Yana a nervous smile. "Wait, did you test yet?"

"I took an ice dance test this morning and passed. My next test is an hour after yours, so I'm going to stay here to cheer you on!"

"Yay! Congrats Yana!"

"Thanks! Now let's focus." Yana instructs. She's like a mini Coach Marie, I think to myself.

Yana takes me, followed by my parents, to a table set up by the entry doors. "You'll want to check in at the table and confirm that you don't owe any money."

At the table, the woman working asks my name and finds me on the list of skaters.

"Is this your first time testing?" She smiles.

I nod nervously.

"I'm sure you'll do great! Good Luck!"

I thank her and turn to follow Yana to wherever she is taking me next. Ah, of course, the locker rooms.

Coach Marie sees us. She gives Tamerah one last hug and squeezes her shoulder while whispering something to her that makes Tamerah nod confidently. Then she jogs over to me and my entourage of Yana, Mom, and Dad.

I'm greeted with a big hug. I don't think Coach Marie has ever hugged me before. This really must be a special event! My coach looks beautiful. Normally she is wearing a big winter jacket and looks like she's cold. Today, she has her auburn hair perfectly done in wavy locks all the way down to the center of her back. Her hazel eyes pop with some magnificently done, but natural-looking eyeshadow and liner. She's wearing dark grey pants and black dress boots with a lovely, soft, cream-colored sweater. She looks like she could be on the cover of a magazine! I can't help but feel proud that she's my coach.

Coach Marie points my mom and dad to the bleachers. "You can watch her test from there, but right now, Khalli needs to focus."

Mom and Dad both give me big hugs and wish me luck. Mom double checks with me three times to make sure I have everything before she heads into the bleachers.

"Dad said he's going to record my test so I can watch it and critique myself later," I tell Coach Marie.

"That's a perfect plan. Then you can see exactly what the judges saw and use their notes to make corrections."

"Make corrections? Does that mean you don't think I'll pass?"

"That's not what I mean at all, Khalli. I think you have a very good shot at this test; you are more than ready. However, just because you pass the test, doesn't mean you are flawless. Good skaters are always making adjustments and fine-tuning their skills so that they are constantly improving. In skating, you're never done learning, there's always room for growth."

I think this means she thinks I'm going to pass. Or is she preparing me to fail. I'm reading into everything way too much at the moment.

"All of my skaters are in this room," Coach Marie tells me as she points to the door to locker room three. "I'd like to keep you all in the same area so that when I need to find a skater I don't need to go on a hunt. Please find a place to drop your things in the locker room and then we are going to warm up."

"Okay!" I go inside, sit down, and begin putting my skates on. After about a minute Coach Marie knocks on the locker room door.

"Are you coming, Khalli?"

"I almost have one skate on, just another minute!" I call back to her.

"Wait! No skates yet! Sorry! I should have been more clear. We are going to get you warmed up off the ice right now. You'll only have a five-minute warm-up on ice, and that's not enough time to warm up your body, that's just enough time to get you used to the ice under your feet and to run through a couple patterns."

Ugh! I take my skates off and hurry out to the hallway to join my coach. She takes me to an open area just outside the lobby where I'll have lots of room.

"We are going to start with a jog." Coach Marie plays some upbeat music over her phone, and we jog together in place to the tempo.

"Next the arms." I watch her as she makes big swoops with her arms over her head and to her sides and do my best to mirror her.

"And now the legs." I follow my coach through a series of exercises all to the beat of her music. After about five minutes, I am feeling completely warm and ready.

"I'm warm!" Coach Marie announces. "Which means you must be warm as well. Are you?"

"Completely!" I promise.

"Awesome, let's get you all stretched out!" Coach Marie helps me stretch my spirals by pushing my leg up and then guides me as I stretch out the rest of my body.

"I'm going to go check the schedule and make sure everything is still running on time. While I do this, I want you to put your dress and tights on. I'll be right back!" And with that, Coach Marie leaves me and I head to the locker room.

I put my tights on and then my beautiful new dress. When I come out of the bathroom stall, I see Yana waiting for me. She must have come in quietly while I was getting ready.

"You look beautiful!" Yana exclaims.

"Thank you! Everyone here today looks amazing, I hope I fit in. Even Coach Marie looks fantastic! Where did she learn to do her makeup so well?" I ask in disbelief.

"I asked her that once too." Yana giggles. "She told me she learned how to do it in the ice show. Coach Marie used to skate professionally, all over the world, in fact! She said she had to have perfect makeup for every show and because of that, she can now do amazing makeup styles incredibly fast. I bet her makeup today only took her five minutes. I wish I could make my face look that perfect in five minutes, or even at all!" She jokes.

"You don't even need makeup Yana. You have the prettiest skin I've ever seen!"

Yana hides her face from embarrassment in her jacket collar but thanks me, nonetheless.

Coach Marie pounds on the locker room door. "They are running ten minutes ahead, time to put your skates on!

Why don't you bring your skates to the hallway so we can talk as you lace them up?"

I rush into the hallway with my skate bag. Oh my goodness! This is really happening! I'm about to test. Oh wow! Oh my! I think I need to pee again. My brain suddenly goes into panic mode.

"Khalli!" Coach Marie must be able to tell I am freaking out. "I want you to focus on putting your skates on right now. Think about how tightly you're pulling the laces, how you're tying them, just focus on what is going on right now and what you can control. And breathe." She instructs calmly. "Once you have your skates on, we can worry about the test. Right now, just worry about your skates."

"I can do that," I say to her and also myself at the same time.

CHAPTER 14

Nerves!

"How are you feeling?" Coach Marie asks me after I am ready to go and wearing my skates.

"Like I'm going to throw up, and like I have to use the bathroom again."

"Sounds about right." Coach Marie smiles. "It's good to be nervous, that means you care. However, it's also important to remember that you are in control of your nerves. You've worked very hard for this, Khalli. You've been at the rink four to five times a week, every single week for the last couple months. You've prepared yourself for this moment. Today isn't about doing anything better than usual or about making corrections. Today is about doing your patterns just like you always do them, the only difference is that there will be fewer people on the ice to get in your way today."

"And judges," I remind her. "The judges are the part that makes me nervous."

"Don't worry a bit about them!"

"What? But they are the reason I'm taking this test."

"That's where you're wrong, Khalli. You are taking this test for yourself, not for the judges."

So she has a point. But I'm still freaking out about the judges.

Coach Marie can read my nerves.

"I'm going to let you in on a little secret, Khalli."

"Okay."

"The judges want to pass you. They want to see you be successful, and they want to see you grow. They aren't looking for reasons to fail you. They are looking to see if you are ready for the next level, and you are. You just need to prove it to them."

"But Yana said they are tough judges and that Tamerah didn't pass," I tell my coach worriedly.

"That is true. However, I can guarantee that I am tougher on you than the judges. If I tell you that your test is ready, you better believe your test is ready!"

Coach Marie gives a pretty good pep talk because I already feel better about what I am about to do. We walk together to the rink doors. There are two skaters left to skate before it's time for my warm up.

"I want you to watch these two tests," Coach Marie insists. What you are about to see is the level two test. This is what I am planning to have you working on already at your next lesson."

"You really do think I will pass, don't you?"

"It would take some seriously major mistakes for you not to."

*****

My five-minute warm-up just started and is going pretty well. There are seven other girls and one boy on the ice with me; all of them are working on the same test. I try not to watch the other skaters and to focus on myself, but I can't help comparing my skating to theirs. One girl has way better spirals than me, but the rest of my skills are better than hers. The boy has very strong and powerful stroking; I hope he doesn't skate right before me!

Coach Marie calls me over to her several times during my warm-up to remind me of little things. "Make sure your knee is straight! Keep your chin up! No toe pushes! Bend down into your skating knee!"

"Why do I feel like my blades are floating on the ice and like I'm not sinking into the ice like I usually do?" I ask nervously. "Is this ice different than the ice at our rink?"

"The ice may be different; ice at different rinks often feels slightly different, but it won't be a dramatic enough difference to change anything about your skating. But there is a very legitimate reason you feel this way."

"Is something on my blade."

"No. It's actually because of your nerves. When your nerves kick in, you will notice you stiffen up and sink less into your knees and ankles. This makes you feel like you are just grazing the ice. I'd tell you to relax a little, but that might not be something you can control just yet. But what you can control is how you think about your skating and your body positions. I want you to think more about your knee bend. Go do another lap of stroking, really thinking about your knee bend."

"One minute!" The referee yells across the ice.

"You only have a minute left to warm up. Let's do that lap now. Don't think about hurrying, think about taking your time and sinking into your knees and ankles. One minute is more than enough time."

I skate to my starting position and take a deep breath. One last lap around the rink before I need to get off the ice. The next time I step back onto the ice, it will be my test.

I push off thinking about not using my toes but rather my full blade. I make sure my back is straight and my chin is up. Now the legs. I press my ankle forward in my boots and bend my knees. Coach Marie was right! This definitely makes it easier for me to feel the ice. I no longer feel like I'm floating or like the ice isn't underneath me. I feel much better and much more in control.

"Please clear the ice!"

All nine of us hurry to the door where all of our coaches are waiting.

"Giana, Mary, and Tyler. You three can wait on the ice." The ice monitor calls to everyone as we reach the door.

The three skaters wait anxiously on the ice at the door while their coaches give them words of encouragement.

"Khalli, step over here please." Coach Marie pulls me out of a moment of curiosity and anxiety as I watch everyone around me.

We've already talked about how this day will work. We've talked about the warm-up, exactly how the test works, practically every little detail. But now that I'm here, it all seems a little bit overwhelming. I guess I forgot about the emotions that would be mixed in with everything else!

"You're in the next group after these skaters. I want you to ignore what's going on out there and focus on what's coming. Okay?"

"Okay." I give Coach Marie a nervous smile.

"All right. Tell me the order of your test."

I list off each skill one at a time.

"Perfect, Khalli. Now, tell me what you need to think about for each pattern."

I tell Coach Marie each skill again and give her a list of things I need to make sure to do. Things like keeping my chin up, sinking into my knees, and more.

"Good! You are so ready for this! Do you have any last questions?"

I think for a minute. "How do I know which judge is judging me?"

"When you skate over to the boards, they will tell you. Just remember to be polite and smile. Also, make sure you thank them at the end of your test."

"And I don't find out right away if I passed, right?"

"Usually not. It often takes fifteen to thirty minutes to get your results."

"Okay. Then I don't have any other questions." I smile nervously.

"That's good, because these skaters are on their last pattern, and you'll be next. It's time to take off your gloves. Do you want to wear your warm-up jacket or show off your gorgeous, new dress?"

I don't even need to think about that one! I pull off my jacket and hand it to my coach to hold.

"Let's do this, Khalli! You are one hundred percent prepared and ready. I know you can do this; you know you can do this. It's time to prove it to the judges!"

"Emily, Khalli, and Davida, you three may step on the ice." The ice monitor directs.

I take a deep breath and turn to face Coach Marie one last time.

"I know you want this. You've worked incredibly hard for this. Now go get it!" My coach gives me a high five, and I skate off to prove to the judges that I'm ready for the next level.

CHAPTER 15

My Time to Shine

"Kaylee? I'm so sorry, how do you pronounce your name?"

The judge smiles kindly at me. She is older, about the age of my grandma. She has short white wavy hair that's poking out around the edges of her maroon hat. She's wearing a thick brown coat with fur on the hood and a maroon and cream-colored scarf. She seems friendly. Well, friendly enough for someone who is going to determine my destiny anyway.

"Ka-lee," I tell her nervously.

"Okay, Khalli. Has your coach told you how this will work?" she asks gently.

"She has. And I know my test order." I tell her as confidently as I can.

"That's what I like to hear! I'll have you get started then. Try to wait for the other skaters so that you are all doing the same thing at the same time. This will keep you from bumping into anyone. Whenever you're ready then," she says with a wide swing of her arm like she's presenting the entire ice surface to me.

I skate nervously over to my starting position. Stroking is my first pattern. I stop completely and turn to see that the judge is watching before I begin. She nods her head. Before I push off, I think through everything that Coach Marie and I talked about and then off I go.

The entire pattern goes so smoothly. On to pattern number two. Again, everything goes smoothly. Pattern number three: spirals. I can do this! I tell myself.

Before I push off, I turn to look at Coach Marie. She encourages me with a smile and nod and then points to her chin and mouths the words, "Chin up."

I smile back nervously as I push off. This is my hardest pattern.

I have to hold my first spiral half the length of the ice rink. I push my knees straight and fight to get my leg as high as I can. I can feel my entire body shaking with nerves and effort. Halfway through! I bend my knees for a big push. Wow! There was some great energy behind that push! I have tons of speed! My free leg stretches to the ceiling, I point my toe and attempt to stretch my leg even higher. Chin up! I remind myself and pull my chin as high as it goes.

I'm three-quarters of the way. I swear this is the longest thirty seconds of my life! I feel my blade wobbling back and forth on the ice; I want to set my foot down. I feel like I'm going to fall. Hold it! I instruct myself, just as Coach Marie has done so many times. Almost there! I cross the thin red line at the edge of the rink. I've made it! I skate around the edge of the rink to finish my pattern and come to a complete stop. When I glance at the judge, I only see the top of her maroon hat. Her head is down as she's writing away. I hope she doesn't have too many bad things to say!

One last pattern. This one is easy for me. I skate to the center of the ice where I usually practice this pattern. Another skater is using my favorite circle. Coach Marie has also made me practice this pattern on one of the circles in the rink corner. I'll just use one of those circles! I turn and begin to skate into the corner and the judge calls my name.

"Khalli?"

I skate over to her.

"I would like you to wait a minute and then use the center circle. I won't be able to see you very well in that corner. The other skater is almost done."

"Okay, I like the middle better!" I say with a smile.

My last pattern is a breeze.

Afterwards, I skate over to the judge. She tells me my test is complete, and I thank her just as Coach Marie instructed.

As I skate to the door, I see my coach beaming at me.

"Khalli! You controlled your nerves very well! I'm so proud of you!"

"Do you think I passed?" I nearly yell, full of excitement and adrenaline.

"I don't get to make the final decision, but I will say I am very happy with how you skated. I saw your nerves come out in the spirals, but you hung on and fought! I love that about you!"

"Thank you!" I give her a big hug. As I let go, I see Mom and Dad rushing over to me.

"You were amazing!" They cheer and hug me. "And you looked so beautiful!"

My adrenaline is still raging. I don't even know what to say, and I can't stop smiling.

"Let's get your skates off, you can also change if you'd like. By the time you're done, your results might even be available." Coach Marie winks.

"Not yet!" Mom orders. "I need a picture of my gorgeous, hard-working daughter with her dedicated coach. Whether you passed or not, you two make a great team!"

Coach Marie and I pose for a picture with the rink in the background. As Mom snaps the picture, someone comes running through with a clipboard full of papers.

"Those are your results," my coach tells me. "But this part now is the hardest part: the waiting game. You won't get the results until someone makes copies. If the copy machine is backed up, it could be a while; but if not, you'll know in less than ten minutes. Go get your skates off, being busy will make waiting easier."

I run to the locker room to take off my skates. I don't want the results to come without me! I pack everything up as quickly as possible and hurry back to my parents and coach.

Coach Marie hands me a piece of paper with a big smile.

"What's this?" I ask confused.

"This sheet of paper is your judge's notes and her decision. Congratulations Khalli! You passed!"

"*EEEEEEEE!*" I jump up and down excitedly. I can't believe it! I passed my first test! I really did it!

Coach Marie goes over the judge's notes with me and explains what everything means and how I can improve my skills. "I'm so very proud of you!" she tells me again.

Mom and Dad give me great big hugs and take turns looking at my sheet of paper. "We should frame this!" Dad insists. "But first, we should go get ice cream!"

"Yes, to the ice cream but no to the framing. At least not this one," I smile with a hint of suggestion. "The last one. When I pass my gold medal test someday. We should frame that one."

Dad smiles at me. "That's my go-getter! And deal! We'll frame that one! Now! On to the ice cream! Snowtop Cream Shop here we come!"

Stay tuned for more of my skating adventures! In just a few weeks, I'll be in my first ice show and shortly after that my first competition. I can't wait to grow as a skater and would love to share my trials and triumphs with you!

Coming soon!

Taking the Ice

Skate Like No One's Watching

ABOUT THE AUTHOR

Allye Ritt was born in Sheboygan, Wisconsin, in 1985. At the age of ten, she began a figure skating hobby that would eventually turn into a lifelong career. Allye is now a seven-time U.S. Figure Skating Gold Medalist, an International Dance Medalist and has also achieved the Skate Canada Gold Dance test. She has skated professionally around the world on three different continents and currently coaches full-time as a career. She is a rated coach through the Professional Skaters Association and also serves as the director for an area figure skating program. Allye thoroughly enjoys guiding her students as they grow in the sport of figure skating and loves watching their confidence blossom as they excel.

In her free time, you will find her in an ice rink, reading, at the gym, or spending time with her husband, Jeffrey, as well as their two cats, Bakyn and Tatyr. As a former middle and high school teacher for German and History, Allye holds a deep passion for learning, especially about historical and modern cultures. This passion has led to a genuine desire to see as much of the world as possible. Together, Allye and Jeffrey love traveling and taking in new places and experiences whenever they have the opportunity.

CPSIA information can be obtained
at www.ICGtesting.com
Printed in the USA
LVHW042346040522
717841LV00049B/2161